Taken by Two Mountain Men

Taken, Volume 11

Jasmine Black

Published by Jan Springer, 2022.

Also by Jasmine Black

Standalone
Shared Boxed Set

Taken by Two Mountain Men

Jasmine Black

Jessie Belle Johnston has always fantasized about being taken by two men but her agoraphobia prevents her from going out and fulfilling her fantasies. Besides, fantasies and reality are two different things...or are they? When the real thing shows up in the form of two hot mountain men at her secluded Canadian Rocky Mountain cabin, Jessie Belle will find out exactly how it *really feels* like to be taken by two mountain men.

Other stories by Jasmine Black include:

Taken by Two Doctors, Taken by Three Doctors, Taken by Two Bikers, Taken by Three Bikers, Taken by Two Billionaires, Taken by Three Billionaires, Taken by Two Bosses, Taken by Two Cowboys, Taken by Three Cowboys, Taken by Two Firefighters, Taken by Two Carpenters, Taken by Two Personal Trainers, Taken by Two Santas, Taken by Two Elves, Taken by Three Bodyguards, Taken by Two Cops, Taken by Two Prison Guards, Taken by Two Lifeguards, Taken by Two Mountain Men and more!

Copyright

Author Note

This is a work of fiction. Characters, places, settings, and events presented in this book are purely of the author's imagination and bear no resemblance to any actual person, living or dead or to any actual events, places, and/or settings.

Chapter One

"**Y**ou're kidding? Troy made a pass at you? I thought those two mountain men were gay?" I asked Chrissy and giggled at the split screen on my computer where my two closest friends, who were identical twins, smiled back at me.

"From the bulges tenting Troy and Bridger's pants after Chrissy politely said she had a boyfriend; they might have been reacting to her hunky boyfriend, whom she'd pointed to at the table where he was waiting on her for her shift to end," my other friend, Megan said and winked.

We all laughed.

The three of us were servers and motel cleaners at the restaurant and adjoining small wilderness motel that Chrissy and Megan's parents owned. The business was on a secluded road, which was an offshoot from the major highway that ran between Banff and Jasper National Parks in the Canadian Rocky Mountains.

The business was isolated and catered to tourists year-round who wanted a remote experience in the Rockies. It was a meeting point for wilderness guides who took their clients into the interior by float plane or interior camping or fishing via canoe on the nearby string of adjoining lakes.

Troy and Bridger stayed at the motel and ate at the restaurant when they came down from their trapping. Sometimes they were gone months on end, living off the land in the mountains, and they'd certainly grown from the gangly pimple-faced teenagers into handsome hunks since I'd seen them several years ago when I'd spent my last summer here at my grandparent's cabin.

I was lucky to have this little stone cabin to live in. It was perched about a half mile up the side of a mountain and a mile from my workplace. So, I walked to and from work and my cabin was rent free, thanks to my grandparents who owned the place and their parents who'd owned it before them.

Unfortunately, I'd had to take a temporary leave from my job because my agoraphobia had returned.

I have an off and on issue of being afraid to leave the safety of wherever I happen to be living at the time my agoraphobia hits. I believe it's thanks to my fighting parents who didn't know any better than to shut up when their three kids were fast asleep. Getting awoken way too many times to high-pitched screaming parents and having things get smashed against the wall on the other side of my bedroom had fried my young nerves. So whenever I got too overtired, my anxiety and subsequent agoraphobia kicked in. Usually I could get it under control before it got too bad, but sometimes, I couldn't.

Complex post traumatic stress disorder was what a shrink had once told me. Well, shit, I could have told him that. He said drugs would help. I tried the drug route but it was too expensive without insurance and I hadn't cared for the side effects, so I'd stopped.

"Hey, are you feeling any better, Jessie Belle? It's been more than a week since you went into seclusion," Chrissy asked, as both my friends expressions grew serious.

"I'm working on it," I lied.

I was still too tense from what had happened to set things off again and didn't venture further than the outhouse or to bathe in a nearby glacial rapids.

"Just keep trying. You've mastered it before and I will keep bringing you groceries until you conquer it again," Meg said with a grin.

She had such confidence in me. I wished I had the same.

"Oh, a reminder," Chrissy broke in, her blue eyes flashing with seriousness. "A bad storm is coming tonight. Your power will most likely go down taking the internet with it. The road up to your place will most likely wash out too, so you might get stranded for a week or two before they fix things. How are you candles and food?"

"My grandparents have lots of candles here and I still have about a month worth of food. You guys are the best, always looking out for me." I replied.

Sure the summer storms scared the crap out of me because the thunder rattled my nerves and reminded me of our noisy abusive household, but this cabin had been in our family for over one hundred years and as Gramps always boasted, no avalanche or landslide had touched it in all that time.

"You're safe there," Chrissy said with a chuckle. "The only other people who use that crazy twisting road are our well-hung gay mountain men."

I laughed, wondering if Chrissy and Megan truly believed those two guys were gay, because they certainly didn't seem that way to me.

"I can come up and get you out before the storm hits. You could stay with Cal and me for as long as you need too," Chrissy offered.

I shook my head as anxiety rushed through me just thinking about leaving the safety of the sturdy stone walls of this cabin and moving in with Chrissy and her new boyfriend.

"I'm fine. Truly," I answered. I would be fine. I'd just pop a sleeping pill. It would relax me.

Both of my friends frowned, probably not believing me.

"Okay. If you change your mind, call before the storm hits. Oh, hey, I hear Cal at the door. Gotta get our supper going. Stay safe, my friend." Chrissy said.

"Bye!" Megan and I called out.

She waved, and then her side of my computer screen went black. Megan was still there, a frown back on her face.

"What's wrong?" I asked as a feeling of unease swept over me.

"I didn't want to say it when Chrissy was here and break her bubble, but those two mountain men are seriously not gay."

I nodded, not feeling in the least bit surprised. I'd never really thought they were into each other, but hey things changed over the years, and they were together in the mountains for extended periods of time. I wouldn't blame them if they had turned to each other for some sexual relief.

"They've made a few passes at me since they've come down from the mountain. I've told them I'm not interested as I have a boyfriend, but they've been asking about you quite a bit," she said.

Surprise hit me.

"Me?"

"Yes. They wanted to know if you have a boyfriend. Where were you? Are you coming back? Stuff like that. But I didn't tell them you are at the cabin. Just that you had a family emergency and had taken a leave of absence. Have they ever made suggestions to you?" Megan asked, a curious expression on her face.

I shrugged.

"The last time they were down, yeah, but I figured they were just playing around. Besides, Chrissy always told me they weren't straight," I admitted.

Megan rolled her eyes and laughed.

"You believed her? Sure, she thinks they are, because that's what our parents tell us, probably to protect us from the rumors."

"Rumors?"

I leaned forward in my chair as fear swept through me.

"They aren't axe murderers, so don't look so worried. Rumor has it they enjoy sharing a woman when they come down from their isolation. With them being up there in the wild, doing that trapping for months on end without female companionship, they get quite horny. When they get back to civilization, they need serious sexual release. I heard that one time they shacked up with a woman for more than a week and all they did twenty-four seven was have sex with her. But you don't have to worry. They're already back in the mountains by now. I heard them talking to dad this afternoon when they came in for lunch. Said they were heading back up tonight to do a bunch of trapping for the overseas market. I figure it will be a couple months before they come back down again."

Mixed emotions sailed through me.

Thankfully, I didn't have to worry about them being killers of people. However I was excited that the two hunky mountain men liked to share a woman after being without sex for so long. I hadn't had sex for quite some time myself, except for some serious masturbating. I'd always fantasized about a threesome, but in reality I knew I would never experience it. It would be too embarrassing.

Megan and I chatted for a while longer before we said our goodnights. Just talking about those two guys though, had gotten me into a hot and horny mood.

It was time to get ready for bed.

A few minutes later, I placed a towel on the floor beneath my feet, undressed at the kitchen sink and began my evening ritual sponge bath.

There was no indoor hot water. Just icy glacial water that came thru a pipe to the tap from a spring on higher ground behind the cabin. While I'd talked with Megan and Chrissy, I'd set a half pot of water to a boil on the stove. Now I placed the steaming pot into the sink and turned on the tap until the water was toasty warm. Then I set the pot on the pine wood counter.

I poured some of that water into the basin and moaned softly as I dipped my hands and washcloth into the refreshingly warm liquid. I soaped the cloth with my planet friendly soap and leisurely massaged my tender nipples and washed along the curves of my plump breasts as I looked out the window at the quiet scenery.

Stunted white bark pine trees grew in abundance at the edge of the yard and up and down the faraway slopes. A few nutcrackers; light gray colored birds with black wings and black beaks, were fluttering around, cracking pinecones and grabbing the seeds inside for food. Golden rays of sunshine illuminated the nearby snow-capped mountains and down below, in the valley, darkness was quickly descending over the lakes and forest as the sun moved behind the mounts. But in the north sky, I spied the dark, threatening clouds of an impending storm. Yup, I would be popping a sleeping pill later for sure.

To my right, perched at the edge of a cliff, the lopsided grey-planked outhouse with the half moon carved into the doorway, stood sentry over the view. I'd already gone to the bathroom before chatting with Chrissy and Megan, so that task was out of the way.

Hurriedly, I soaped the rest of me, rinsed with some fresh water and towel dried. Then I grabbed a glass of ice-cold water from the tap and headed to the bedroom.

Time to masturbate!

Chapter Two

The cabin only had two rooms. One room consisted of the kitchen, dining room and living room and the second room was this bedroom. None of the windows had any curtains, as there were no neighbours up here, except for the road about a quarter mile away that the mountain men used to go up to a parking area. But that road was rarely used and you couldn't see the cabin from there.

So I pretty much walked around nude inside and outside the building whenever I wanted to, which was often.

The bedroom was shabby but cute, about fifteen feet by fifteen feet and it was still decorated the way Grand and Gramps had left it before they'd retired to travel the world. The scratch and dented cedar wood panelling had seen better days and the brown-colored wool rugs on the floor were old. The best features in the room were the antique white iron wrought Queen sized bed along with matching white night tables on each side of the bed and a couple of white dressers.

I hadn't the heart to remove the framed family photos hanging on the walls of when my mom and my uncle vacationed here with their parents when they were kids. It appeared they had happy times up here. They were always laughing in the pictures.

There were faded color and black and white, eight by ten-inch pictures of them blue berry picking, sledding in the summer, and swinging in a tire hung from a rope on a branch over the river. I have no idea why my mom ended up being such an angry bitch, but she certainly didn't get her alcohol and anger issues from my kind grandparents. Dad, on the other hand, had a quick temper and a rotten family upbringing, so that could account for his drinking.

Whatever their issues, the damage had been done to me and my anxiety and agoraphobia was a side effect. Thankfully though, my sexuality was very much alive.

Eagerness had me hopping into bed. I spread my legs, snuggled the cozy down comforters up to my knees and switched on the hurricane style lamp beside my bed. Then I slid open the drawer, withdrew my bottle of sleeping pills, my special cream and my vibrator.

I placed the cream and vibrator beside me, quickly popped a pill and down my glass of water.

By the time the sleeping pill kicked in, I'd be finished with my battery-operated boyfriend and ready for la la land.

I smiled at my vibrator.

"Hey, big guy, you and I are going to have some fun tonight fantasizing about our mountain men, aren't we?" I asked.

The machine was a charming thing. It was in the shape of an eight-inch long and two-inch-thick pale pink penis complete with plum shaped cockhead massager and clit stimulator.

I lay back against my pillows and turned on the machine. It pulsed warmly in my hand. With my other hand I cupped my left breast and began to rub the vibrating cockhead over my left nipple. I inhaled at the instant throbbing sensations it created. My burgundy-colored nipple immediately blossomed into a rosebud shape and it ached pleasantly as it grew taut.

My breathing quickened. I moved to my other breast, cupping my hot flesh and rubbing the vibrator over my nipple. I watched it darken in color and bead. Felt the quivering sensations begin between my thighs.

I fantasized that my two mountain men were here on the bed with me. Troy on one side, Bridger, on the other side. Their hands cupping my breasts, their hot mouths sucking on my nipples.

Heat burst through me as I kept vibrating my nipples, back and forth I went, until they grew so tight, they hurt.

Time for my soothing cream.

I flipped off the vibrator and set it upon the bed. Then I unscrewed the lid of my special cream. I'd bought it along with some toys just before moving here, knowing any online orders would be coming to my workplace and I hadn't wanted anyone to find out about my naughty side, so I'd stocked up.

I knew I was asking for it in using this cream and I didn't use it often, but tonight I just wanted that extra oomph.

I dipped two fingers into the cool balm and slowly massaged it over my rigid left nipple. The coolness felt like bliss as I rubbed and pinched my sensitized flesh. Then I scooped out more cream and massaged it over my other nipple and down along the curves of first one breast and then the other.

Soon wherever I'd smeared the cream, my flesh began to tingle and grow quite hot. I began pinching and pulling my nipples, bringing the pain and pleasure that I craved. I moaned as both my breasts soon felt like they were on fire and my nipples were tiny flames sticking straight up into the chilly air.

I smeared some cream on my lips, loving how they soon began to grow hot and tingly. I fantasized that one of my mountain men was kissing me. His firm lips melting over mine with possession.

Then I dipped a finger into the cream again and scooped out a generous amount. I spread my legs wider and moved my creamed finger between my thighs.

I sighed as I gently rubbed the silky cream all around my clitoris until my vagina went wetter and my clit grew ultra-hot and tingled. Then I grabbed my vibrator, smoothed a bunch of cream onto the cockhead and using the cockhead massager, I began to massage my tender clit with torturously slow motions, loving the arousal I created.

I created a stimulating friction, concentrating on increasing the pressure on my little bundle of nerves until a sizzling hunger erupted throughout me. My thighs and lower belly tightened.

I widened my legs even more and arched my back as I kept massaging first one and then the other tingling nipple, with my free hand, and imagined Troy, one of the mountain men, touching me there. With my other hand I circled the massager around and over my clit, imagining Bridger, the other mountain man, was dropping his big body between my thighs, his big cockhead teasing my clitoris, and his hot mouth kissing my tingling lips as he held himself over me.

Then I dipped the vibrating cockhead into my soaked pussy, pretending a giant hot penis was entering me. My vaginal juices were flowing nicely and the vibrator slid in easily, pulsing against the sensitive muscles that eagerly clenched the thick intrusion.

Then I withdrew, kneaded my clit some more until the arousal sent my senses into hyper drive. My breaths quickened and I plunged the vibrator deep into my pussy like a strong cock would do. Then I withdrew it, quickly moving the cockhead over my sensitized clitoris again, until it pounded with tremendous heat and tingled insanely from the cream.

I felt my control slip.

Oh yes, having two mountain men making love to me with this cream would be ideal.

Just thinking about them made me cry out as convulsions swirled out of nowhere. I jerked and enjoyed the erupting pleasure. I plunged the vibrator back into my clenching vagina and heard the slurp of my juices with my every thrust.

Pleasure wrapped around me like a vice. I shuddered and cried out as the spasms made love to me. Moaned as I gyrated my hips and thrust the hot vibrator in and out, my pussy greedily sucking with need.

I shuddered inside the orgasm. Loved the raging pleasure as it sank deep within me.

I twisted, moaned, and cried out as I shook and gyrated and imagined Troy and Bridger here with me.

While the pleasure roared through me I vaguely noticed the bedside light go off, thrusting my room into darkness. Thunder roared in the distance, but I just kept fucking myself. This was too good to be stopping now.

I convulsed and looked straight ahead at the window where lightning flashed, briefly illuminating my room. I imagined the two mountain men's faces right there at the large window watching me. Troy with his chestnut brown eyes and Bridger with his forest green gaze. I knew it had to be just a sleeping pill illusion. But man, I had one hell of an imagination because I swear they were both grinning with appreciation.

As I stared at their faces, I just kept moaning and gyrating and twisting within the waves of pleasure. Kept thrusting and pinching my nipples and massaging my breasts.

The orgasm was long. It went on forever and I loved it.

Perspiration blossomed over my skin and yet I just kept looking at my two imaginary men who seemed so incredibly real as they watched me writhing, bucking and thrusting that vibe into me like a woman possessed.

They were both shirtless in the window. Muscles bulged in their big shoulders as they moved their arms. I knew what they were doing. They were masturbating while they watched me masturbate.

I moaned at that thought and just kept pistoning the vibrator and loving my breasts with my other hand. Soon the incredible spasms began to ebb and then I finally stopped thrusting.

Wow, that had been so intense and was I ever getting sleepy and ultra-relaxed.

I panted as I withdrew the toy, tossing it somewhere beside me. That naughty cream was still working heat and tingles through my intimate areas so I kicked away the comforter and just kept my thighs wide open, allowing the cool night air to breathe against my hot pussy and breasts, and so the men could see.

They simply kept staring at me and continued their masturbating. I watched them for awhile. Their shoulder muscles and biceps bulging as their arms moved faster and faster.

Slowly my eyes drifted closed. I smiled as I heard first one of them moan as they came, and then the other groaned as he came.

Yup, I sure did have one heck of an imagination. Then, I fell asleep, knowing my dreams would be filled with hot hunks and sizzling sex.

Bang. Bang. Bang.

A knocking sound at the door crashed me out of a hot sex dream and thrust me into reality. I opened my eyes and stared into the cold darkness.

I blinked into the desolate darkness trying to figure out where I was and what was going on. Cobwebs dragged at my thoughts and the familiar anxiety twisted my stomach. My heart cracked against my chest like a battering ram.

Dad and Mom were fighting again? Seriously?

I was cold and shivering. Must have thrown off my blankets.

I reached down and pulled up the covers right beneath my chin and shivered from both fear and at being cold. Impatiently I waited for what was to happen next.

What had woken me up? Had Mom thrown Dad's whiskey bottle at the wall? Or had Dad whipped Mom's wine bottle right through the living room window like he'd done so many times?

I froze as the bang, bang, bang came again. It was followed by a rumble of thunder.

Oh no! I burrowed deeper into my pillows, searching for some kind of comfort.

Lightning flashed at the bedroom window illuminating my surroundings and I suddenly realized I wasn't a kid anymore. I wasn't at home in that cesspool. I was at Gram and Gramp's cabin and the storm was here.

And someone was knocking at my door? What the fuck?

Chapter Three

I gazed at my illuminated windup clock. It was a little after midnight. I had slept maybe two and a half hours.

Had Chrissy decided to come up to get me? No, it couldn't be her. She would have called out, letting me know it was her. Unless I'd been sleeping so deeply I hadn't heard her?

I lay in bed and waited. My teeth were chattering now as the fear zipped through me. Who was knocking at my door?

I heard nothing more.

Suddenly rain slashed against the windows, lightning sizzled brightly at the glass panes and thunder crackled nearby making me cringe. I closed my eyes and sank even deeper against my feather pillows.

Man, I hated loud noises. Sure, I could use ear plugs. But I couldn't stand things in my ears.

But had I imagined someone had been knocking? Maybe the sleeping pill was screwing with my mind? It did that sometimes. I mean, I'd sure imagined those mountain men earlier while I'd been masturbating.

I swallowed and listened. Nothing else happened.

I began to relax and allowed the sleeping pill to work it's magic again. I must have been dreaming or having some weird complex post traumatic stress flashback or something. I debated getting up and going to take a look, but I figured if someone had been around, surely I would have heard something more.

Then I brightened as an idea hit me.

Of course! It was probably just the park ranger coming by to tell me the roads were sure to wash out with this rain and if I wanted to leave with him. He was such a sweet elderly man. Always looking out for me. He knew I was alone here and had given me his personal phone number saying if I ever had an emergency to call him or his wife, Helga.

And if it had been someone else, they surely wouldn't be stupid enough to be hanging around in this downpour. The porch had a bit of a cover, but it had a major leak and wouldn't keep one dry for long.

Okay, all was good. It was just thundering now. Nothing more. Thankfully, I had taken that sleeping pill because my eyes were feeling so incredibly heavy again.

I closed my eyes and found myself thinking about my past and how I'd ended up here living like a freaking hermit, just wanting to be left alone.

The instant I'd had hit eighteen years old, I'd quit high school. I'd only had a couple of months left before I would have graduated, but I'd just needed to get out from under my abusive parents reign of terror. It had broken my heart to leave my two younger brothers behind stuck in that mess, but I knew if I'd stayed in that environment I would either have become an alcoholic like my parents, or whatever was left of my nerves would be completely gone and I would have either killed myself or ended up in a looney bin for the rest of my life.

So yeah, being half sane was better than being insane or dead.

I was fortunate that I'd found plenty of under-the-table work, where my employers paid cash. I'd mostly cleaned houses, walked dogs, baby sat for friends, and crashed on friend's couches while I saved my money. As I accumulated work experience and references, people stopped asking if I had a high school diploma. That's when I was able to move from friends' sofas into cheap apartments and I began waitressing, being a short-order cook, or motel house cleaner.

I was now twenty-four and considered myself a Jane of all trades. I was very proud of my accomplishments. The problem was every once in a while my anxiety got the better of me and I just started having panic attacks and needing to stay indoors and away from people. I had hoped coming out here to the scenic mountain cabin with the fresh, crisp air and being with my childhood friends, Chrissy and Megan, it would help me, but I was slowly coming to realize that wherever I went the problem would be with me because it was *inside* me.

I was broken.

Not only was I emotionally broken, but I was also a workaholic. I had no boundaries regarding work and with it being the high season at the restaurant and motel down in the valley, I'd taken on too many hours, filling in for others who went on summer vacation. I'd neglected my diet, skipped meals, slept less and worked more than I should have because I wanted to make as much money as I could for the just-in-case days I had no money.

I blew out an irritated breath. Yup, and now because I was filled with anxiety again, I was making no money. Well, wasn't that a bad pattern. I would have to re-evaluate my priorities. But first of all, I needed to get back to sleep.

Tomorrow, I would start on a plan that I could put into motion about having more me-time and less work. I just didn't know what me-time would involve.

Not yet anyway.

WHEN I WOKE UP THE next morning, bright sunlight streamed into the bedroom and instantly I realized I felt cheerful because I had slept through the storm. The clock was showing eight o'clock and the air was cold. Unfortunately, the bedside lamp was still off. That meant I had a power failure on my hands. I'd have to cook breakfast on the woodstove, but that was okay. I'd done it many times in the past.

But first, nature was calling.

Quickly, I got out of bed, opened the window to get in some fresh air and shivered as the frigid mountain breeze slapped against my bare flesh. I threw on my robe and slipped my feet into my sandals.

Despite it being chilly in the cabin, I felt so refreshed from the good night sleep that I'd forgotten what had happened last night with someone possibly lurking around. That is, until I opened the front door on my way out, and a package just a bit bigger than the size of a shoe box, fell into the room.

Someone had propped it up against the door, making sure I didn't miss it.

A mail delivery? In the middle of the night? Here?

So, that's what it had been. I *had* heard someone!

Shit! I didn't know if I should be relieved at discovering I hadn't imagined the knocking or be scared that someone had been prowling around. Who would be nuts enough to be coming here in the middle of a thunderstorm to bring me something? Had the girls decided to pop up with more food even when I told them I had enough?

I shook my head as I lifted the package and placed it on the nearby living room table. The box was too light and too small to contain groceries. My name wasn't on it either. There was no writing at all. The package was wrapped in plain brown packing paper and it had been slipped inside a transparent plastic bag so it wouldn't get wet.

So, why knock on my door and scare the daylights out of me?

Some idiot, that's for sure.

I would open the package when I returned from the outhouse.

The air was unbelievably scented this morning as I strolled across the yard. I could smell the tangy aroma of pine from the nearby trees. Flowery smells from the abundance of purple fleabane and yellow asters edging the path permeated the air and there was a wet dirt smell of moss that grew on the nearby rocks. From the north angle that the gentle wind was blowing, I could feel the icy air coming off the nearby glacier. But the sun was just popping over the nearby snow-capped mountain tops. The rays were strong and hot and I knew it was going to warm up very quickly around here.

I bundled my robe closer around me and hurried to the little outhouse. After I did my business, I admired the cabin as I made my way back toward it.

The cabin walls were built from slabs of shale and limestone. The windows were wood framed, the thick frames painted an emerald green. At each side of each window there were workable wood shutters that were painted black.

The steep angled roof had been constructed from pine logs and there had been wooden shingles but I remembered when I was a kid, my grandparents had nailed old, corrugated sheet metal over the top of the rotting shingles to keep the weather out. But there were rusty spots here and there on the metal and it was just a matter of time before the rest of the place would start leaking, just like the porch. I'd have to let grandfather know the next time I got a chance. He'd know what to do.

After I went inside, I quickly built a small fire in the woodstove to chase away the chill. The warmth made me feel less wary about having had an unexpected visitor and so I settled on the sofa and stared at the surprise package.

Who had brought it? Who was it from? What was inside?

Carefully, I slid it out of the plastic bag and then ripped open the tape and paper. I frowned as a shoebox emerged. Someone had brought me shoes? I shook my head and lifted the lid.

Shock washed over me as I peered inside. What in the world?

I reached in and withdrew the many packages of flavored, colorful condoms and packages of adult toys. There were several assorted sizes of smooth, metal butt plugs, nipple clamps, labia clamps, bondage ropes, and a black blindfold. And then I lifted out a gorgeous cream-colored nightie. Well, nightie might be the wrong word as it was entirely mesh, see-through with low V-neck and the sides were completely open with only a belt at the waist to keep the garment secured. The material was soft as satin and delicate flowery lace edged the bottom and side hems.

Appreciation whispered through me. I don't think I'd ever seen anything so beautiful, or so sexy in my life.

At the bottom of the box was a note.

I held my breath as with trembling fingers I lifted the note out of the box. I didn't recognize the handwriting but it was definitely a man. The letters were bold and confident.

We thought you might find these useful.

Until we meet again,

Troy and Bridger

p.s. We enjoyed last night.

My mouth dropped open as surprise and embarrassment washed over me.

What I had thought was my imagination or a drug induced figment of my imagination had been real! The mountain men *had* been outside my bedroom window last night watching me masturbate!

Oh my God!

Chapter Four

My face heated so much, I thought for sure my cheeks would explode into flames. Obviously Troy and Bridger knew I was staying here.

Fear skittered over my nerves. I needed to call Megan and Chrissy and tell them what was going on. I found my cell phone on the kitchen table where I had left it. I turned it on and quickly realized there was no signal. The cell tower was out.

Panic sifted through me.

Crap. With the power out, no Wi-Fi either, so I couldn't contact them via my computer.

I could walk out of here.

Hurriedly, I dressed and headed outdoors.

A few steps beyond the porch, I quickly stopped as my familiar anxiety grabbed hold. My heart was racing. My chest went tight and I found it difficult to breathe.

My legs and hands began to shake as I stared down the dirt driveway. It wavered in the heat. Or was I wavering?

Okay, just keep calm. Nothing bad is happening. You're just having a bit of a panic issue.

If those men wanted to do something to me, they would have easily broke in the door and had their way with me.

They had spied on me though, through the window. Watched me masturbate, for heaven sakes. What kind of men did that? And I had fallen asleep, naked. My legs spread wide to their view. What kind of woman did that? Obviously, they thought it had been an invitation.

I just needed to chill. Had they any ill intent, they would have come into the cabin. Maybe they had, and I hadn't heard? I *had* taken a sleeping pill.

My nerves were seriously getting rattled just thinking they might have been in there, until I remembered what Megan had said. They would be gone for months. She'd heard them tell her dad there were trapping for the overseas market and were in the mountains.

Well, the mountain part was true. But they hadn't been trapping last night.

I headed back inside and instantly began to feel better. I plopped down on the sofa and stared at the arrangement of toys.

Okay. They had left me this present, complete with condoms. Because....?

They wanted to have sex with me when they returned.

Could I do it?

When Troy and Bridger had hit on me in the restaurant just before I'd taken my leave of absence, I'd thought they were so cute. So grown up compared to the serious teenage boys I'd hung around with during summer holidays here with my grandparents. Having them hovering around me while I'd served their meals at the restaurant and having them asking questions if I had a boyfriend, if I wanted to date them or if I wanted to join them for drinks after work, had made some naughty desires stir deep inside my pussy at the idea of having sex with one of them.

But I'd played mysterious. Not answering their questions. I'd remained as professional as possible.

And last night Megan had mentioned the rumor about them sharing a woman...

Heat flushed through the rest of me and my pussy quivered with need. I felt hot between my legs. Wet, just remembering how I'd pistoned that vibrator in and out of me like a woman possessed.

I trembled and blew out a tense breath. This was so not good.

Here I had fantasized about having a ménage some day and the opportunity was staring me right in the face and I was panicking. I really should get out of here. But I couldn't leave.

I was caught between experiencing a ménage or a panic attack. How crazy was that? The answer should be a no brainer.

Food. I needed food. I always could think better on a full belly.

AFTER FORCING DOWN some toast and coffee, I was once again staring at the note Troy and Bridger had left.

Until we meet again.

I gazed at the butt plugs. A couple of them were *huge*.

Okay, they must know it would take days or maybe even weeks for me to get to the largest plug.

I had time.

Time to decide, time to panic, time to fantasize, or time to make an escape plan?

But first, time to relax and enjoy one of these plugs. It had been a couple of years since I had worn one. Longing swept through me. I had gotten used to wearing one in the past. Could I do it again? Even if it was just for fun for now?

Besides, I was kind of mentally trapped here, even if the road hadn't washed out.

I grabbed the smallest packaged plug and ripped open the plastic. I removed the plug and headed into the kitchen. The water left over from the coffee had been boiled. I used that and some soap to thoroughly clean the plug. Then I brought the lube and plug into the bedroom with me.

A little while later, I had the toy inserted. My anal muscles eagerly clenched the toy and I smiled.

Muscle memory.

My ass remembered Jackson pistoning into me. His harsh grunts as he'd pleasured himself, had sometimes, okay, many times, pissed me off, because the guy just didn't seem interested in giving me an orgasm. But I rarely complained. I was a people pleaser. Their pleasure came before mine.

I frowned as something inside of me shifted.

When was I going to put my needs first, damn it? Other people put their needs first. Why shouldn't I?

From what I remembered from my teenage years, Troy and Bridger had always been perfectly well-behaved boys. They hadn't tried to cop a feel, snapped the back of my bra strap or violently yanked on my hair or the other not so pleasant things like the guys in the city had done to me to get my attention.

Megan, Chrissy and I and the two guys had just swam, hiked, kayaked, canoed or fished. We'd laughed, told jokes or invited each other over for campfire cookouts.

We had all been friends. Every summer we had just picked up like friends.

Until I hadn't returned here for several years. We'd all grown up.

So, I guess I did know them. Just not intimately. Well, that wasn't true, now was it? They had seen me last night in my birthday suit.

Hell, yes, for the first time in my life, I was going to please myself. I was going to wait for them to return and then I was going to make sure they did to me what they had done to that other woman over the course of more than a week. Twenty-four hours, seven days a week of sex!

Whew! Just thinking about it had my ass clenching the butt plug, and my pussy getting tense.

In the meantime, I was going to work on a me-time routine and begin to do some inner trauma healing as per what a shrink had once suggested by reading some of those books I had purchased in the past and hadn't yet read.

And when those two mountain men came down from the mountain. I was going to get myself pleasured with a hot ménage à *trois*!

The days and nights whizzed by fast. Too fast.

I did a lot of reading, lying in a hammock in the cool shade of two large pine trees in the yard. Self reflection was the name of my game as I delved deep into my emotions, tapping into numerous traumas.

And I really *felt* my emotions. I cried like I had never cried before. I would find my inner child from a certain trauma, visualize myself being there and I would soothe her and emotionally hug her and hug myself.

While comforting myself, I realized I had felt abandoned as a kid because my parents never really were there for me. Their bottles of booze where their babies, not me or my brothers. When something bad happened to me, like I got bullied at school or my cat died, they weren't emotionally available to comfort me.

Because my parents were neglectful, a lot of the work fell upon my young shoulders. Taking care of my younger brothers, doing the laundry, going to the corner store for meals that I could cook out of a box for us because my parents were too drunk to cook.

It had been bad and I'd never told my grandparents. How weird was that. I'd protected my parents, my abusers.

Now I was an adult and I could dive into my traumas, self soothe and comfort my inner child and then let the trauma go. And if my self soothing didn't work on one trauma, I would try and try again until I was at peace with it.

Sometimes anxiety overwhelmed me, but I could *feel* myself healing. I was freeing myself.

One day, I realized I was happy. Go freaking figure. I'd found a way to self partner with myself.

Sure. I had a long way to go. There were a lot of traumas to dredge up. Plenty of self healing to do. But confidence was edging out my fears.

I just knew I was touching the tip of an iceberg.

After two weeks the electricity returned and I had Wi-Fi again, a day later my cell phone was working. Everyone was missing me at work and I felt like I wanted to be with people again. I returned to work a week later, walking along the road, to and from work, skirting around the giant gulleys in the road or hiking into the thick forest to bypass the washouts.

At work, I began to make boundaries, saying no to extra hours. It felt good to gain control and stop pleasing people. I needed to take care of myself because I now realized no one else would.

Chrissy and Megan and I began to go to Banff together to do some shopping. Sure, my anxiety sometimes still overwhelmed me, and I would excuse myself and go to the bathroom or just wait for my break at work, then delve into the emotion I was feeling at the time and self-soothe. It wasn't a self-talk thing. It was a tapping into my emotion, visualizing what trauma might have been triggered and soothing myself thing.

I had good days and bad days, and I got better at self-partnering the more I practiced.

I was being my own hero. I was gonna make it through life. I just knew it.

On my first weekend off work, I decided to go to the secluded swimming hole on the river where Chrissy, Megan, Troy, Bridger and I used to swim when we were teens. We'd had fun times. It was the same place my mom used to come with her brother and parents. The tire hanging from the tree I'd seen in the photographs on the wall, was gone, but the memories were still here. If I listened hard enough, I could hear our laughter.

It was rolling toward October and the days were shortening and getting colder, but today the sun was hot and high in the sky, towering over the immense green forest of pine trees that cradled the blue-green river. The heat beat down on me as I undressed.

Chapter Five

I knew no one was around. I'd swam here several times since moving into my grandparent's cabin and there had never been another person here. The public didn't know this swimming hole existed, hence why I wore my birthday suit.

The sun reflected off the lazy-moving water, making it look like sparkling white crystals had been tossed across the surface. It looked pretty and it made me feel peaceful and calm. I stood there, at the edge of the river, my toes digging into the warm sand, the hot sun needling my flesh.

When I felt like I was boiling, I took a deep breath and dove into the water. Icy tendrils wrapped around my heated flesh, and I came up gasping and swearing.

Damn, but the water was ice cold!

But so refreshing too!

In order to warm up, I vigorously swam around the swim hole, thinking about Bridger and Troy.

A couple of months had gone by since I had found that package propped against my door. I had never told Chrissy or Megan about it. I wasn't even sure now that it was an invitation to me. Maybe the two men had just wanted to unload the stuff before heading into the mountains and they'd somehow seen my bedroom light from the road as they drove by and come to take a look?

I'd graduated to the biggest butt plug. It fit snugly in my ass today as I swam. I was wearing it, just for fun. Just in case...

Every night I tried to masturbate my mountain men out of my mind, but I hadn't been able to. If I knew where they were up in these mountains, I would go to them and demand they make my scorching fantasy about them sexing me twenty-four seven come true.

I laughed at that thought, flipped onto my back and floated out of the swim hole into the river. I looked up at the towering snow-capped mountains that peeked over the tips of the pine trees. The mountains were all around me and they made me feel safe. I just had the feeling I was going to live here forever.

After awhile, I swam back up the river to where I'd left my things.

As I stepped out of the water, I froze.

My clothes were gone! Nothing had been left behind but my shoes.

I swallowed as both fear and excitement rocked me.

Had a grizzly bear somehow managed to steal my clothes? Or had the mountain men finally returned?

To say that I was a little pissed off that I had to walk through the woods back to my place wearing no clothes, was an understatement. Good thing it was a warm day.

But I kept expecting a growling grizzly bear to jump out at me from behind a tree with my ripped clothes hanging between its jaw. Or maybe someone else had taken my clothes besides my mountain men? Some deranged killer who was watching me right now?

My heart sped up at those thoughts and I felt a bit relieved as I neared the cabin.

Visually I checked for signs the mountain men might be here. What I found were my clothes, neatly folded, on the lone porch chair. A note had been tucked beneath my panty.

Jessie Belle,

Tonight. You won't need your clothes if you want us.
If you want us to come to you, leave the porch light on.
After that, there is no turning back.
Until we meet again,

Troy and Bridger.

My mouth went dry. I wasn't sure if I should be scared or thrilled that it had been those two who'd taken my stuff. I was trembling as I scooped up my clothes and scurried inside. I only locked the door at night and it appeared nothing had been disturbed in the main area of the cabin.

But I could smell *they* had been here. A whisper of fresh scented soap hung in the air.

Instincts told me to go into the bedroom. That's where I found another note laying on the bed. My heart was crashing as I read the words.

Jessie Belle,

If you want us to make love to you, tonight, then trust us and tie yourself with the binds as best you can and don't forget to wear the nightie and blindfold.

Remove your butt plug.

Until we meet again,

Troy and Bridger.

Have mercy! I suddenly realized the bindings they'd put into the package were now attached to each bedpost. The black blindfold and that gorgeous negligee that had come with the package lay on my pillow. They must have noticed the butt plug packages had all been missing.

Those mountain men had been here among my things and they were starved for sex.

For a split second, the urge to run and get out of here snapped through me. But I held steadfast. This was my fantasy. This was my place. No one was going to frighten me away.

I had some serious decisions to make. And I needed to make them by tonight.

THE PORCH LIGHT WAS on and twilight dangled over my cabin as I stood in front of the full-length mirror hanging on the inside of the bedroom door. I'd brushed my auburn hair until it shone, whispered some rosy blush on my cheeks, curled on some black mascara making my eyelashes look twice as long and dashed a healthy dose of red lipstick on my lips. I looked ready and available for sex.

Then I focused my attention to the cream-colored negligée I wore. The low V-neck showed off the deep valley of my breasts, the see-through mesh illuminated my curves and showed off my nipples. I'd tied the belt around my waist, pulling the front closed, but the sides were completely open, exposing the sides of my breasts, my waist, hips and long legs.

The material felt like the soft petals of a flower embracing my body and delicate lace edged the bottom and side hems.

I was seriously stressed with my decision. What if I didn't like a threesome? I mean, I'd removed the plug and my ass felt so open and waiting to be filled, but what if my body parts had problems accommodating their body parts?

I caught my gaze in the mirror. My brown eyes stared back at me. I looked like a deer caught in the headlights and I found myself laughing.

What an idiot. My fantasy was about to become reality, and I was shitting myself. I should consider myself lucky that two men wanted to ease me into this fantasy turning reality.

A brief flicker of wondering how Bridger and Troy would know I wanted a ménage whispered through my head. The only ones I'd told were Chrissy and Megan and that had been only once when we'd been discussing our sexual fantasies one night when they'd slept over the night before I'd started working in the valley.

They wouldn't dare say anything to the guys. It was just a coincidence. The thought that my friends were somehow behind this vanished just as quickly as it appeared.

I nodded to myself, gathered my courage and lay on the bed.

In a few minutes, I had the binds secured around each ankle and one wrist. With my free hand, I managed to slide on my blindfold. It wasn't easy, but I did it.

Now, I waited.

My breaths came fast as I listened to every sound in the cabin. The tick tock of my bedside clock. An owl hooting somewhere outside. The cabin creaking as it settled in for the night.

Earlier, I had stoked the wood stove. I could hear the occasional crackle and pop of the fire. It was relatively warm in here as I had left the bedroom door open and the heat was slowly making its way in. Or maybe I was just hot with excitement?

Suddenly a new noise whispered through the air.

I tensed.

Men's voices. And they were coming toward the cabin.

I forced calmness into my being and suddenly realized that yeah, I was ready for this ménage.

But my face grew hot as the front door creaked open. I'd left it unlocked for them.

The two men were whispering now.

My breath lodged in my throat as I thought I heard the rustle of clothes being removed. Unexpectedly I felt overwhelmed with thoughts of how crazy this seemed. I'd barely chatted with them in the restaurant months ago and now this.

"Jessie Belle, are you sure you're okay with this?" I heard Bridger call out from the other room.

Good heavens, they still had those boyish manners!

I tried to answer, but I could only croak.

Quickly, I cleared my throat and called out an affirmative.

The tongue and groove pine floorboards creaked as they walked across the living room and then into the bedroom, their steps quieting on the carpet. I could feel both of them staring at me, standing there, their hot stares taking in my bound body.

"You look very pretty in that negligee," Troy said softly.

"I knew she would," Bridger added.

"Thank you," I whispered.

I grew alert as their footsteps approached the bed.

The mattress to my right dipped. I inhaled and smelled that fresh soapy scent that I had smelled earlier when I'd returned to the cabin to find my clothes outside.

"I didn't appreciate my clothes being stolen," I blurted, trying to keep my voice cool, but it came out bedroom breathy.

"We saw you coming to the swimming hole, so we scrambled out, grabbed our clothes and hid. We didn't want you to see us just yet. If we had, we would have taken you right then and there," Troy said from right beside me.

Sweet mercy!

"You looked breathtaking as you stood there at the river's edge. Naked and raw in the beauty of nature," Bridger said in a hoarse voice. He was still standing away from the bed.

My face heated even more.

"You were watching me?" I exclaimed.

"Wasn't the first time," Troy answered. He sounded gruff.

My mind flew back to that night when they'd been watching at the window while I'd masturbated.

Chapter Six

"You looked so damned hot with that vibrator thrusting in and out of your pussy. Had we come inside and taken you then, we knew it would have been a mistake. We'd heard you were dealing with something personal," Bridger said.

I nodded but didn't tell them about my agoraphobia. I could tell them some other time.

"We knew you were living here. I mean the place does belong to your grandparents," Troy said as he bound my free wrist with his big strong fingers.

"But Megan said you were asking where I lived? And that you were hitting on her? And on Chrissy?"

I inhaled sharply as Troy's hot hand cupped my right breast and he tweaked my nipple. Arousal quickly arrowed through me. Because of the negligee's mesh material, I could feel the callouses on his fingers.

"Don't believe everything that Megan and Chrissy tell you, Jessie Belle," Troy whispered as he kept kneading my nipple, creating a fiery tension there.

"That's right. Chrissy's boyfriend, Cal is a good friend of ours, we sometimes just play with her in the restaurant making her think we're hitting on her. Cal has a fetish. He gets sexually excited when guys hit on his girl. We were just doing him a favor," Bridger explained.

Oh my gosh, I wondered if Chrissy knew that about Cal.

"But they said you both had hard-on's?" Oh, had I just said that out loud?

"We've always got hard ons, baby. And Megan has a loose tongue when she's drinking in the bar. She flirts too much too. She also confessed to us early on that your fantasy is a ménage. She knows we are interested in you and only you."

That bestie bitch of mine! She had lied about the guys hitting on her? Was she jealous? No, if she'd been jealous she would never have mentioned them having sex with another woman. Unless she'd wanted *me* to be jealous and stay away from them? And she did have a habit of bar hopping. I'd been invited to go with her early on when I'd moved back here, but I'd firmly told her I would never drink alcohol or step into a bar because it reminded me too much about my alcoholic parents. I refused to go down that road for myself.

"And you can believe the rumors about us wanting some hot and heavy sex after we come down from our trapping. Our fantasies of what we'll do with a woman is what keeps us hot during those long, cold lonely nights. We've been doing a lot of fantasizing about you, Jessie,"

"Sex for as long as you can stand it. And for as long as you can stand," Troy whispered in my ear.

I creamed at his words.

Oh my goodness!

"Bridger, go on and get those other supplies we discussed, would you? I'll keep her warm," Troy said.

"I'm on it," Bridger replied. I heard his footsteps head back out of the bedroom.

Nervousness tugged at me. Now that they had me fully bound, I was completely at their mercy.

"W-what other supplies?" I muttered.

"You'll see, J.B., but in the meantime..."

I tingled with delight as he said my nickname. The guys had nicknamed me J.B. and I'd forgotten all about that.

Man, I sure was glad I'd come back here!

The mattress moved and then Troy's warm breath caressed my cheeks. A moment later, his mouth slid over mine in a possessive kiss that shocked my senses and literally made my toes curl.

Then his scorching tongue pressed against my lips and I automatically opened to him. He stroked into me and incredible sensations exploded through my body as he touched his tongue to mine.

I moaned my appreciation.

He stopped tweaking my nipple and his hand slid over to my other breast. He began pinching that nipple, which grew hard and throbbed as he created pleasure and pain.

His tongue wrangled with my tongue, forcefully mating with me until I felt a powerful surge of pleasure, which arrowed down to between my thighs. I creamed. Hard.

Instinctively I jerked against him, wanting more of what he was giving.

He withdrew and began nipping at my lips with his teeth. They were sharp little stings that had me gasping and pulling against my restraints. Then he licked the stings with his rough hot tongue, caressing them and making them feel so much better.

"Looks really sexy, with you kissing her like that," Bridger's deep voice sailed through the air breaking me from the pleasure Troy was creating.

I groaned my disapproval when Troy suddenly stopped kissing me.

"I see we're ready for what's to come," Troy whispered against my ear. I shivered as he licked my earlobe.

He continued tweaking my nipple and my breaths were coming fast and hard.

The bed dipped between my spread legs and then Bridger's hands slid beneath my hips.

"What's going on?" I whispered.

A pillow was thrust under my ass, lifting my pussy and bottom upwards.

"You'll see, sweetheart. Believe me, what we have in store for you is well worth your patience," Bridger said in a promising tone.

Suddenly I wished the blindfold was gone. I wanted to see what was going on.

The mattress moved again between my legs and I had the feeling Bridger was climbing between my spread thighs.

I held my breath as the hem of my negligee was lifted. Warm air breathed against my quivering pussy as hot, strong hands tucked the silky mesh material of my negligee in and around my waist. My ass and pussy were now fully exposed for them.

"She's ultra-beautiful," Bridger whispered.

Troy's hand flew off my breast. I could feel him moving away. A moment later, I knew Troy was having a good look between my thighs.

"Very nice. And her ass is fully open and waiting for us," Troy acknowledged.

"Yes, very nice, indeed. She's creaming too. But that pubic hair has to go as we need a very succulent contact there. I have all the shaving utensils ready. Let's get started, shall we?" Bridger replied.

Oh my God! They were going to shave my parts down south? I'd never shaved myself there. Had never thought about doing it. Bridger's words bounced around in my head.

Succulent contact, he'd said. They had to be talking oral.

Sweet mercy! I'd never experienced oral sex before.

Curiosity grabbed hold of me as I heard the tinkle of water. I gasped as a warm washcloth was draped over my mons and labia areas. The warmth felt nice, really nice.

After a minute, the cloth was lifted away. More tinkling of water. The warm cloth was placed upon me again.

"We stayed away from you as long as we could, Jessie Belle. I hope your issue has been resolved? If not, we would be more than happy to help," Bridger was saying from between my thighs.

Oh great. Conversation with two men ogling my intimate parts? Like, seriously?

"I...I'm fine. Working on something. But I'll tell you guys about it sometime," I breathed.

For a moment I was embarrassed about my anxiety and agoraphobia issues, but I slammed hard on that thought. There was nothing wrong with letting them know at another time. Nothing to be ashamed of. I was mentally broken and I was in the process of healing.

It was kind of like a broken leg that needed to be mended. My problem would just take more than six weeks in a cast and months of physio because I'd endured abuse pretty much my entire life. Something like that took patience and time to heal from.

"Not a good time?" Troy chuckled from the area of my nightstand. I heard him pull open the drawer where I kept my naughty stuff. In my minds eye, I could see him checking out my vibrator, the tingling cream I sometimes used and I had a dildo in there too.

"She has better things on her mind," Bridger said, coming to my rescue.

He removed the washcloth and I stiffened when I felt the mattress moving again.

"Just a bit of shaving cream. It's actually whipped cream. I beat it outside the instant we saw the porch light go on. Whipped it up with our rotary hand beater, especially for you. We don't have electricity in the mountains, so sometimes we whisk up some instant pudding for dessert. But with taking you for dessert, delicious cream is extra special," Bridger whispered from between my legs.

Something cool and foamy was lathered over my mons. I became quite focused on where Bridger touched me when his male fingers pulled on my outer labia and cream was dabbed here and there and pretty much everywhere down there.

"A work of art," Troy complimented. He'd moved to my left side now and the bed dipped as he sat down. Or maybe he was lying down beside me?

"Hmmm, we're going to need to figure out a way to get you out of this sexy apparel, aren't we? Get some whipped cream onto your nipples," he said.

He was close now. Very close.

My cheeks flushed hot. Whipped cream on my nipples!

I could hardly wait!

"Ah, now I remember why we got this negligee with no sides," Troy whispered in a thick voice. His fingers untied the sash and then I felt the material being lifted. Warm air breathed against my left breast.

"A dollop of cream, right...here," he whispered.

I gasped as he placed some frothy cream upon my throbbing nipple. A second later, he was cupping my breast. His hand was gentle as he held me and then he began to lick and slurp the cream. The heated warmth of his tongue made me ache as tension built. My nipple hardened beneath his rasps and it felt like it was growing to two times it's size.

My breathing grew deeper and faster and I felt my vagina cream.

Then he moved his mouth away and I clenched my fists in frustration.

While Troy added more cream and then licked and slurped some more, Bridger began to shave me!

The pleasure and pain Troy created had me wanting to buck and jerk, but I needed to be careful and I forced myself to remain still and simply experience what the two men were doing to me.

Every time the razor touched my skin, I held my breath. This was new to me and I wasn't sure what to expect. But the razor moved cautiously over my mons and every so often I heard the tinkle of water as he rinsed the utensil. Then he placed more cool cream upon my hot flesh and continued his ministrations. Before long, I wasn't afraid he might cut me, I just needed to remain as still as a corpse.

The two men remained silent as they worked on me. Pray tell, I sure didn't want to interrupt and break their concentration.

I loved the sultry pull of Troy's' mouth upon my nipple and enjoyed the tender way Bridger shaved. There were exquisite touches on my labia as he took one between his fingers and pinched my flesh as he moved my pussy lips this way and that as he shaved, then rinsed.

The more Bridger touched me, the more I could feel the muscles in my lower abdomen tighten with eagerness.

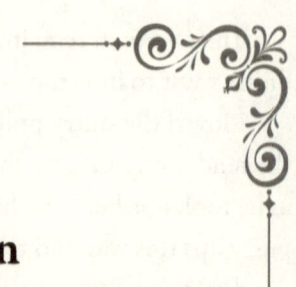

Chapter Seven

My inner thighs were beginning to tremble too and I was growing hot and impatient as my pussy began to feel so wet, heavy and hungry for impalement.

Just the thought of one of these men powering into me had me moaning aloud.

"And now for dessert," Bridger whispered as he wiped me down with a wet cloth.

I held my breath as he then once again sensually smeared whipping cream all over my mons and on and around my labia. My hands clenched and I fought for control as he placed a cool dollop on my sensitive clitoris.

I yelped as a moment later his tongue licked the cream off my clit, but he did so ever so gently, too damned gently, leaving me feeling needy and impatient. I grew feverish and I wanted to yell at him to hurry up and suck my clit until I orgasmed, but he pulled away.

"Heavenly delicious," Bridger murmured against my pussy. I heard him smack his lips together.

Dear me! He was acting as if I was a feast!

"She is, isn't she," Troy said softly from around my nipple. He sounded as if he were dazed.

Suddenly, I became incredibly aware of the solid, heated length of Troy's erection as it pushed up against my left hip.

So I had been right in hearing the rustle of clothing after they'd entered the cabin.

Troy *was* naked and his penis was unbelievably blistering against my flesh. I imagined how engorged it must be as the blood pulsed along his shaft, lengthening and thickening. How the veins would be interwoven, bulging with arousal and his cock purplish with desire.

Troy's hand was kneading my breast now as he suckled my nipple, drawing and pulling, bringing a fiery need throughout me. The pulsing pressure of his scorching mouth, had me gasping and shuddering.

Bridger began licking at the whipping cream he'd placed on my mon, his tongue a hot flame as he brought me to the edge of excitement. The long, carnal strokes of his tongue moved closer and closer to my clitoris, making me whimper with anticipation.

I tensed as Bridger sucked one labia into his mouth, pulling and swirling his tongue around my tender flesh. Then he let go and sucked on my other pussy lip. The act had my body awakening as it had never awakened before. Every nerve ending flared to life. The bristles from his facial whiskers rasped fire wherever he touched and every time he pulled away I cried out my frustration.

Then he'd dab more cream upon my pulsing pussy. Licking and lapping, the slurping sounds just about driving me mad. Instinctively I bucked as his tongue began to circle my tender clit. I felt the ache in my vagina grow even more with that desperate need to have a cock thrusting into me.

Bridger backed off with his tongue and then smeared more whipping cream onto my mon, around pussy lips and clitoris.

I suddenly realized the two men were controlling me with their tongues. Controlling my need for release. They were slowly bringing me toward the climax I was now craving so much that my body felt as if it might detonate and blow apart if I didn't have their cocks.

How long would they keep this up? Would I go mad enduring this torment? What had I been thinking accepting bondage so easily? Being tied down was making me nuts!

My mind flew to what Megan had said about them fucking a woman twenty-four seven for over a week.

Oh dear Lord! What sexual torture had I signed up for?

"It was nice watching you masturbate that night, Jessie Belle. Real nice," Bridger said from between my legs.

A momentary embarrassment rushed over me, and then it was gone. I didn't have to be ashamed of masturbating in my own bedroom. They'd been the peeping Toms. Any embarrassment was on them and it appeared they wouldn't be apologizing for trespassing anytime soon.

"I'm glad you enjoyed yourselves," I answered in as cool a voice as I could gather.

I blew out a tense breath as Bridger began licking me again. Closer and closer he lapped to my swollen clitoris. And then he was there.

I cried out, my hips arching off the pillow as his mouth suddenly fused over my tender bundle of nerves. He lapped at my clit, teasingly dabbing his tongue like a fiery flame until my senses became overwhelmed. My vagina clenched and my pussy juices once again spilled out of me and into his mouth.

Yet, I couldn't orgasm. He wasn't bringing me far enough. The bastard knew what he was doing, that's for sure and I now realized those two teenage boys I'd hung around with...the ones with the manners...were no more.

I could feel Bridger's fingers now, digging into my flesh as he gripped my quivering hips. He held me down and he just kept sucking my cream out of me.

Oh God, it felt so good to be sucked down there, but so bad too. I wanted it to keep going, but I also wanted him to stop.

Come on! I need to come!

My body pulsed beneath his mouth. I could hear the blood rushing in my ears. Could feel my breasts enlarging, my pussy dropping and opening, my ass clenching.

Everything felt so swollen, so needy. And incredible sensations were sparkling all through me too. It was like a pleasure war was brewing inside me. I knew I was close to release. I knew they were in control. Had it been me masturbating, I would have brought myself to satisfaction long ago.

I could hear myself start to scream inside my head. To beg them to take me.

Out loud, I called them devils. Bastards. Gods.

And then Bridger stopped.

"You like that, J.B.?"

"I...yes, please. More! No, take me!" I gasped as confusion rocked me. I wanted them to keep going, yet I wanted to orgasm.

Man, I couldn't even think straight. My brain was fragmenting.

"What do you say, Troy? Should we give her more?"

Troy let go of my nipple with a pop.

"She'll be coming twenty-four seven for the next little while, I'm sure she can stand to wait just a little bit longer? I need to change sides and I found something you can use on her too," Troy growled.

No! No more waiting!

"Please, please take me," I gasped.

The men ignored me as I lay there shuddering and waiting.

The mattress stirred as Troy got off. I sensed him moving to the foot of the bed where he hesitated a moment.

What had he found for Bridger to use on me? What was happening? Damn blindfold!

I sensed Troy moving to the other side of the bed. The mattress dipped as he lay down beside me. Once again I felt his thick erection pressing against my hip.

Oh man, I was craving his shaft bad.

Gosh, the imprint of his penis felt so incredibly hot against my flesh. But I *needed* his cock plunging inside me!

"Oh wow, look what Troy found," Bridger suddenly teased from between my legs.

"What?" I snapped.

"Now, now, Jessie Belle, we'll put you out of your sexual misery...in time," Troy whispered as he lifted the side of my negligee revealing my breast to him. A second later, I felt a dollop of whipped cream drop onto my nipple.

Oh no! I was suffering and they were keeping me from the pleasure I craved.

"Your pussy is nice and bare and juicy too. I'm sure you must feel a most intimate contact now that all your hair is gone," Bridger murmured from between my thighs.

"Please..." I begged. I swear I was going to lose it.

Bridger chuckled.

He kissed my mons and then licked my clitoris again and again, slowly, seductively, until I was trembling from the onslaught of pleasure and need.

Troy was whipping my nipple again. Slurping off the cream, moaning as he nibbled, creating such an erotic friction with his lips and tongue that my pussy was once again creaming!

I swore and yanked against my restraints, finally having had enough.

Troy stopped and chuckled.

"Wow, the she-cat's claws are coming out! You look so hot when you're mad," he said.

His cavalier comment in ignoring my needs, pissed me off.

"When I get out of these binds, you two are going to—"

Hot lips fused over my mouth and my senses went spiralling as Troy kissed me with such possession and control, I saw beautiful silver stars in my minds eye.

A second later, Bridger's hot mouth melted over my pussy and he began sucking my juices.

Instantly I was on fire.

The heat of arousal rushing through my system was insane. My pussy was inflamed beneath Bridger's mouth and my breasts heaved as I kissed Troy back, despite my anger.

The man knew how to kiss. Knew how to make me quickly forget that I was pissed off.

Then Bridger's mouth moved away and I felt something thick and soft, and lubed slide into my vagina. Instantly I knew what it was.

It was my pink vibrator with the massaging cockhead and the clit stimulator. He'd put plenty of that naughty tingling cream on it. The machine happily hummed and vibrated erotically as Bridger gently thrust it in and out of me, making sure the clit stimulator massaged me perfectly. Making sure that naughty cream went into me nice and deep.

I could already feel it working its pulsing magic. Growing hot and tingling deep inside of me until I writhed and moaned.

My climax was coming closer and closer.

My inner thighs tightened even harder. My belly clenched.

"Let's see how you like it when I'm thrusting this vibrator in and out of you, like a real cock," Bridger purred.

And he did thrust. Once, twice and three times.

And I exploded.

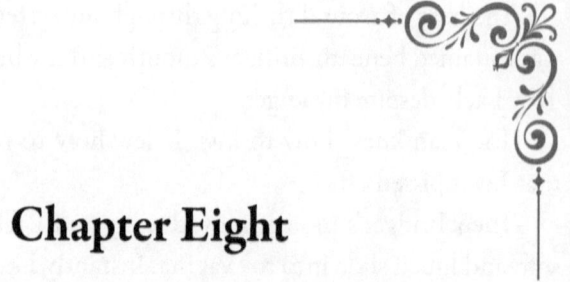

Chapter Eight

The pleasure was brutal. It was beautiful. And it struck my body and my senses with incredible speed.

In an instant I was riding such unbelievable waves of pleasure that I could actually visualize myself on an ocean, wrapped inside huge sparkling white waves. They punched pleasure into me, around me and over me. The thrashing sensations were sharp and tight, wild and wonderful as they pummelled me, stroking and plunging and loving me.

Bridger kept thrusting my vibrator in and out of my vagina, driving those magnificent convulsions as I bucked and writhed against my restraints. My vaginal muscles were clenching and spasming all around each impalement.

I could feel the quivering of the vibrator every time it plunged into me. The delicious thickness, the satisfying length and the hot tingle of the cream deep inside my vagina as it worked its magic, seducing my inner muscles, making them clench even harder.

Every thrust was another sizzling shock bringing more sensations and more convulsions. Fiery heat raged.

This was the best orgasm ever and I just kept rolling with the tumultuous waves. Gasping and keening and loving it.

By the time the incredible spasms and pleasure ebbed, my body felt slack and satisfied. I was covered in perspiration and panting so hard I thought I might collapse from the insane deep breaths.

Bridger had stopped thrusting the vibrator and Troy had stopped kissing me. I could hear Troy breathing beside me. Could feel Bridger's hot breaths against my pussy.

"Man, that looked like it was good for you," Bridger praised.

"It was exceptional," I confessed in a breathy voice I didn't even recognize.

I felt heady with excitement and now understood why they'd waited so long to make me come. So much pent-up tension had to go somewhere and have mercy, did it ever! The blindfold had made me concentrate on the sounds and my feelings. I'd internalized everything and it had been so well worth it.

I wanted to do it again.

"I need to take her," Troy whispered from beside me.

"So do I," Bridger answered.

My thoughts swirled as there was a sudden flurry of movement. My restraints were being loosened and then they were gone.

Hard hands wrapped around my wrists, helping me to get up off the bed and to stand on my unsteady legs.

"Since we know this is your first time. We'll go nice and slow," Bridger announced.

My senses were once again going into overdrive. They wanted sex. Both of them. Of course.

I'd been selfish, wanting my desires to be met. I'd forgotten about their needs. They needed their release too but the orgasm that had tore through me had left me physically exhausted. I trembled as I stood there, but thankfully someone from behind was holding onto me. It had to be Bridger. I recognized his breathing. Raspy and deep. I could feel his body heat wafting off him and splashing against my trembling flesh.

Renewed desire began to throb inside of me. The craving for another climax was suddenly calling out to me again.

Yeah, I wanted another orgasm. Just like the last one.

"Here are the condoms," Troy said from in front of me. His voice sounded harsh, thick with arousal.

"Hold yourself steady on Troy for a minute," Bridger said as he let go of me.

I wobbled at my newfound freedom. Spread my legs, steadied myself and reached out.

I touched Troy. There were hard muscles everywhere on his body and I slid my palms over his rugged taut belly, loving the way he was groaning as I settled my hands upon his strong hips.

It was kind of hard trying to figure out what I was doing with the blindfold on, but I decided to leave it on. It seemed to give me a laser focus on things.

The tear of plastic soared through the air from behind me and in front of me.

Then came the rip of foil as the condoms were unleashed.

Troy hissed and I imagined him sliding the protection onto his engorged penis. Then his hands slid onto my waist, holding me steady.

The slap of whipping cream or maybe lube upon Bridger's cock as he stood behind me.

Bridger's calloused hands grabbed my hips. I tensed as he pressed his large cockhead against my sphincter. Despite my nervousness and the tension growing through me, I was surprised that my ass opened to him so easily and he slid in.

He was thick, oh so thick. Smooth as silk and hotter than an inferno. He didn't push in too far, just enough to bring a beautiful pleasure burn that had me gasping.

My anal muscles protested as he sank in deeper. I moaned at the pressure but I loved the incredible feel of having his cock buried in me. It was like I was his possession. Like I was being branded as belonging to him.

Then he withdrew.

And I felt empty.

I wanted him back inside me again. But I had to be patient. I understood what they were going to do to me.

Double penetration.

My pussy felt so hot and heavy. So empty as I waited for Troy.

His breaths grew heavier as he held me tight.

"You are so beautiful. I think you'll be just as beautiful when you are ninety years old. I've always thought that way," Troy murmured.

My heart smiled at his compliment. I'd had no idea he felt that way about me. But ninety years old? Seriously? The man was delusional.

Suddenly his mouth melted over mine, once again shocking my senses into overdrive. I gasped into his mouth as he thrust his cock into my wet vagina in one rough plunge.

Mercy! He was *so* big!

Troy withdrew and then Bridger thrust his cock into me. It was a slow thrust and just a bit further in than the last one. I could feel his every elevated vein, every delectable inch of his swollen flesh as it jerked against my stretching anal muscles.

Then he was gone and Troy pistoned his shaft into me again, pushing me closer to the pleasure I wanted.

I moaned my appreciation into Troy's mouth. He kissed me harder, then withdrew his penis.

And so it went, one man powering into me and the other man leaving. They quickly got into a rhythm that speared spasms and pleasure into me. They had me writhing between their hot, sweating bodies in no time flat.

Their shafts were long, thick, and hard as spikes as they pistoned. They just kept going and going, gathering speed and intensity. Soon they were entering me at the same time. Their swollen shafts pummelling and stretching my inner muscles like they'd never been stretched before.

I just couldn't get enough of the heat, the raw friction and the harsh yet succulent way each of them ground their strong bodies against me and drove their hard-as-a-rock cocks into me. The slaps of their flesh against my flesh flew through the bedroom air. Their groans mingled with my moans as they pushed me closer and closer to my climax.

My lower belly clenched with erotic tightness, my legs quivered and my nipples felt so exotically sore as I rubbed them against Troy's hairy chest. I dug my fingers into Troy's hips holding on tight as both men rode me.

Every stroke of theirs went deeper and deeper into me driving the pleasure and the pricks of pain higher and higher. Their cocks were like heat seeking missiles and then I ignited into a firestorm.

The orgasm tore through me, tightening my entire body with exquisite pleasure until I was shaking and convulsing and crying out my release into Troy's mouth.

They fucked me through my entire orgasm and then I could feel their release as they shivered and quaked against me, their moans guttural and wild as they unleashed their hot seed into their condom-sheathed rods within me.

When the pleasure ebbed away I was barely aware of their hot cocks leaving my satiated body. Of being lifted into someone's arms, carried to the bed and then the cool sheets melted against my hot, wet back.

Someone removed my blindfold, but I just kept my eyes closed, languishing in the sultry aftereffects of my release. My pussy continued to spasm gently and my breathing was slowing down.

I felt the bed dip on each side of me and I loved how both men snuggled against me, their body heat keeping me nice and toasty. Then the comforter embraced me and I slept.

The next morning sunlight streamed through the bedroom window and bathed my body in extreme heat, waking me up. I blinked at the stinging yellow light and lifted my arm up above my eyes to shade out the sunshine. For a minute I didn't remember what had happened last night, but as I gazed down at my breasts which were uncovered due to the comforter being draped around my tummy, I could feel my nipples had been used wonderfully. They were plump and pink and pleasantly sore.

I also realized my mountain men had left the bed as I was alone. I smelled the tangy aroma of bacon and the tart smell of coffee. My tummy growled and my mouth watered. I was hungry.

But holy cow! I'd had my first ménage and it had been better than I had ever fantasized.

My first instincts were to just lie here in bed and go back to sleep and rest up for more sex, but the lure of the delicious fragrances of food wafting in the air had me leaving the bed and putting on my robe.

As I entered the other room, I found my two mountain men, sitting silently at the kitchen table.

They were completely naked and they looked incredible. Both wore five o'clock shadows over the lower half of their faces. Muscles bulged everywhere on their bodies and it appeared they'd bathed because their hair was damp.

Suddenly Bridger turned and saw me. His dark eyebrows raised in surprise.

"Ah, she's awake," Bridger said with a smile that got my heart pumping and my pussy and ass clenching in remembrance.

"She's brunch!" Troy growled as he turned to look at me. His green eyes flared with arousal.

He was about to stand up, when Bridger grabbed him by his arm, stopping him cold.

"She needs to eat. And then after she's fueled we will take her again."

Oh my goodness! Heat fused my face and my body.

It appeared I was suddenly going to have agoraphobia again. At least for the next little while.

I'd just have to let my employers know about that issue that had suddenly popped up because I certainly couldn't tell them the truth that I was being taken over and over again by two mountain men.

The End

Spunky Girl Publishing Catalog

Jasmine Black
~Erotica~Without the Romance

Here are some more Jasmine Black eBooks...

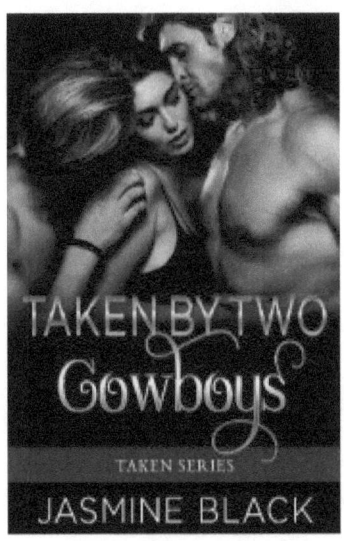

Taken by Two Cowboys

Sierra Allan works hard at her late-father's horse ranch. When her step-brother adds her handy girl services to a private auction to help raise money for the failing ranch, she figures there's no harm...but she's stunned when her services are sold to two sexy cowboys who give her an erotic way to save the ranch—submitting to their dark desires..

Taken by Three Billionaires

Billionaire friends, Liam, Theo and Elijah have just won Princess Isabella in a billionaire card game. Isabella knows exactly what the three men will want from her...she just hadn't expected to have all three of them at once!

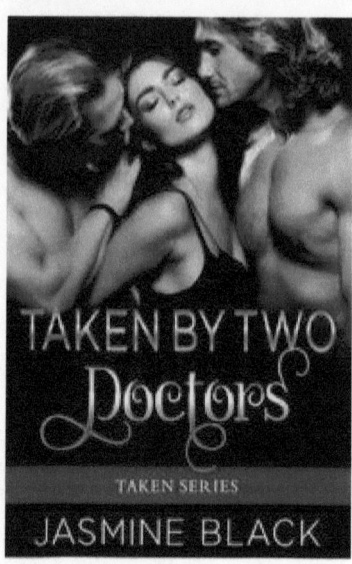

Taken by Two Doctors
A BDSM Medical Fetish Erotica Quickie MFM

━━━━◦◦◦━━━━

Waitress Jean Spelling visits her controversial doctor once a month for some much-needed...stress relief. She looks forward to putting her feet up in the stirrups and enjoys Dr. Ball's naughty unconventional treatments. This time when she arrives, she's surprised to discover that she'll be physically examined by two doctors and they'll prescribe her some much-needed release right there on the examination table!

eBooks in Jasmine Black's Ménage series
Taken by Three Bodyguards
Taken by Three Bikers
Taken by Three Billionaires
Taken by Three Doctors
Taken by Three Cowboys

eBooks in Jasmine Black's Taken series
Taken by Two Prison Guards
Taken by Two Elves
Taken by Two Mountain Men
Taken by Two Cops
Taken by Two Santas
Taken by Two Lifeguards
Taken by Two Firefighters
Taken by Two Bikers
Taken by Two Billionaires
Taken by Two Bosses
Taken by Two Cowboys
Taken by Two Personal Trainers
Taken by Two Carpenters

Jasmine Black Website ~ http://www.jasmine-black.com
Twitter ~ @blackerotica1

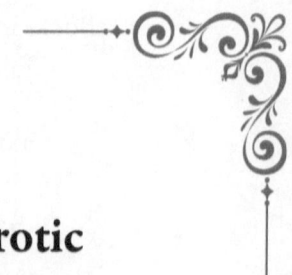

Jan Springer ~ Erotic Romance ~

~
Cowboys For Christmas
Cowboys Online 1 ~ Moose Ranch
Jan Springer
A Canadian Contemporary Ménage Romance m/f/m/m Series

Jennifer Jane (JJ) Watson has spent the past ten Christmases in a maximum-security prison.

The last thing she expects is to get early parole, along with a job on a remote Canadian cattle ranch serving Christmas holiday dinners to three of the sexiest cowboys she's ever met!

Rafe, Brady and Dan thought they were getting a couple of male ex-cons to help out around their secluded ranch, but instead they get an attractive and very appealing female.

In the snowbound wilds of Northern Ontario, female companionship is rare.

It's a good thing the three men like to share...

They're dominating, sexy-as-sin and they fill JJ with the hottest ménage fantasies she's ever had. Suddenly she's craving cowboys for Christmas and wishing for something she knows she can never have...a happily ever after.

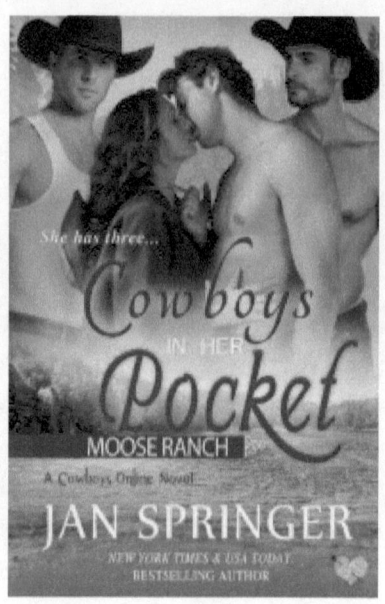

Cowboys In Her Pocket
Cowboys Online 2 ~ Moose Ranch
Jan Springer

After spending ten years in a maximum-security prison Jennifer Jane (JJ)
Watson got early parole and a job on a remote Canadian cattle ranch
playing housekeeper to three of the sexiest cowboys she's ever met...
Spring has finally arrived at Moose Ranch, and a single woman fresh out
of prison shouldn't be experiencing scorching ménages with her three
sexy-as-sin cowboys. But JJ's love for her men continues to grow as she
gives into the fevered heat and scorching passions she feels for each of
them.
Life is perfect.

Until her new life is tested when mysterious happenings occur on the ranch and then one of her cowboys is viciously attacked and injured.

Will JJ's newfound freedom and happiness be ripped away?

Rafe, Brady and Dan never expected to find an attractive and very appealing female to help them out at their secluded ranch. But in the wilds of Northern Ontario, female companionship is rare. It's a good thing the three men like to share...

Brady, Dan and Rafe have never been happier. Their cattle ranch is flourishing and their continued desire to share the sexy woman who cares for them makes their life complete. Until danger threatens to rip everything apart...

Loving Her Cowboys
Cowboys Online 3 ~ Moose Ranch
Jan Springer

After spending ten years in a maximum-security prison Jennifer Jane (JJ) Watson got early parole and a job on a remote Canadian cattle ranch playing housekeeper to three of the sexiest cowboys she's ever met...

Her love for her cowboys continues to grow as she gives into fevered heat. But JJ's simmering restlessness explodes and she's seriously making up for lost time by pursuing her dreams. There's only one little problem. She hasn't revealed to her bosses what she's been up to while they're away tending to the cattle. She knows when they discover her secret, there will be hell to pay.

Ranchers Rafe, Dan and Brady have found the woman who completes them. She makes their secluded ranch a home-sweet-home. She's vulnerable, sweet and willing to share her bed with all three of them. But when JJ's secret is unwittingly revealed, they're stunned and angry. They figure it's time to dole out some fiery punishment in some mighty naughty ways...

Cowboys In Her Heart
Cowboys Online #4

After spending ten years in a maximum-security prison, JJ gets unexpected parole and a job on a Canadian ranch serving up scrumptious dinners and lots of hot love to three of the sexiest cowboys she's ever met.

Jennifer Jane "JJ" Watson has never been happier. She's going to have a baby!

Thankfully, their wilderness ranch is a nice distraction for her three sexy cowboys while she's away flying her plane. But when she's home, her dominant hunks are tending to her naughty pregnant cravings and that includes plenty of sizzling ménages.

Rafe, Brady and Dan don't much like the idea of their woman flying the Canadian skies and being at the mercy of the unpredictable Northern

Ontario weather. They would prefer having her warming their beds twenty-four seven. But she has a way of getting what she wants and right now she needs her new-found freedom.

Worst fears are realized when JJ, her friend and JJ's plane suddenly go missing and she doesn't come back home to them.

Always Her Cowboys
Cowboys Online 5 ~ Moose Ranch

1

Reader Advisory: Best to read in order. 1. Cowboys for Christmas, 2. Cowboys in Her Pocket, 3. Loving Her Cowboys, 4.Cowboys in Her Heart, 5. Always Her Cowboys. 6. Her Forever Cowboys 7. Claiming Her Cowboys

---

A Canadian Contemporary Ménage Romance m/f/m/m
Jennifer Jane (JJ) Watson has spent ten Christmases in a maximum-security prison. The last thing she expected was to get early parole, along with a job on a remote Canadian cattle ranch serving Christmas holiday dinners to three of the sexiest cowboys she's ever met!

---

1. https://janspringerauthor.files.wordpress.com/2017/11/alwayshercowboys_ebook-1new.jpg

Rafe, Brady and Dan thought they were getting male ex-cons to help out around their secluded ranch, but instead they got an attractive and very appealing female. In the snowbound wilds of Northern Ontario, female companionship is rare. It's a good thing the three men like to share...

Christmas is coming once again to Moose Ranch and with JJ's due date approaching, she's distracting herself from anxiety attacks by keeping herself ultra-busy preparing for the arrival of her baby and planning Moose Ranch's first annual Christmas party!

In having a wee baby on the way, there's a lot of stress for Brady, Rafe and Dan. Especially due to JJ's decision on having a wilderness mid-wife deliver the baby *at their secluded ranch* - with *all* of them present for the birth! But their concerns don't stop the men from showing JJ how much they love her...out of bed and in!

With wicked snowstorms, a grounded bush plane, a cheerful holiday party and a sweet baby on the way, the owners of Moose Ranch know this will be one sparkling Christmas season they won't soon forget...

PLUS: HER FOREVER COWBOYS ~ Snowy Creek Ranch #1 Cowboys Online #6

Claiming Her Cowboys ~ Moose Ranch #6 Cowboys Online #7

Risqué Girl Delights Boxed Set
(Contemporary Erotic Romance)

2

...a touch of romance, a ménage or both?

Edible Delights

Years ago Allie Masters lost herself in the scorching passion of a ménage a trois relationship with her two bosses. In order to regain her independence, she walked away.

Max and Nick were very fulfilled with their gorgeous assistant. The lovemaking was breathtaking and both men willingly shared the woman they wanted to spend the rest of their lives with. Then she left.

Now Max and Nick have decided it's time to seduce Allie back into their lives.

Toygasm

It's a case of mistaken identity when the two owners of Sexy Toys, show up for an erotic several day photo shoot of their toys with famous nude model Cammie Creek.

Cammie believes the two hunks are the male models she's supposed to work with. Usually she doesn't mix business with pleasure, but when they're seducing her right there in front of the camera, she can't resist turning them into her own personal naughty toys.

Josh and Jode are enjoying the perks of being male models; hot lust, sizzling toys and the best pleasure they've ever had. But how will Cammie react when she discovers they're actually her bosses and not just male models?

Shy Girl

Finally free of an abusive relationship, "Shy Girl" Emma McCall sheds her inhibitions and explores her sensual side at Club Rendezvous, a club specializing in the Alternate Lifestyle.

At the club she's surprised to find Logan Masters, a sexy hunk she's secretly fantasized about since college. With Logan's help, Emma will experience her ultimate fantasy - a scorching ménage a trois.

Risqué Girl Delights Boxed Set Con't

Roman and Julietta
Her perfect lover...

Modern day pirate Julietta Black's life has always been immersed in the violent and traditional ways of piracy. When her family's arch enemy puts a hit out on her family, Julietta knows there's only one way to lift the hit; she must kidnap the enemy's sexy grandson and force a union between the two warring families. Night after night, wrapped in Roman's strong arms, she can't deny the searing attraction blazing between them. Nor can she deny he now holds her heart as well as her life in his hands.

His dream angel...

When Roman Prince's mysterious captor offers him a luscious woman to bed, fierce desire ignites, melting his usually tight self-control. Lust quickly turns to love as he enjoys their naughty trysts more than he should. How will he react when he discovers he's been kidnapped, not for a ransom, but captured for his sperm?

Alpha Outlaws Boxed Set (Books 1-5 Outlaw Lovers)
5 Books!!

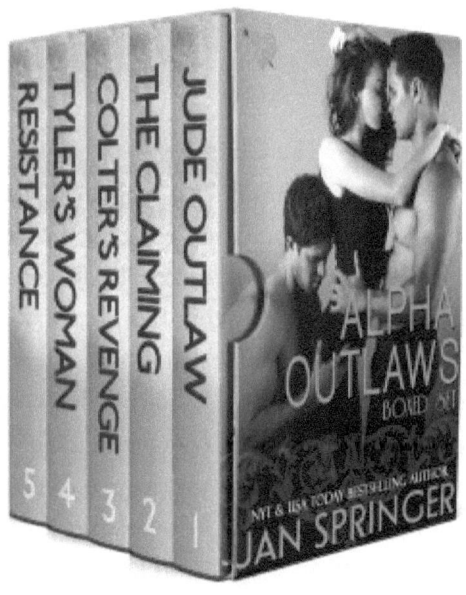

3

In a world gone mad...
A fast-acting virus has killed a majority of the world's female population.
With the creation of The Claiming Law, groups of men suddenly have the
right to claim a female as their sensual property and the sexy Outlaw
brothers are going to declare ownership of the women they love...any way
they can.

Jude Outlaw

When Cate Callahan learns Jude is coming home from the Terrorist
Wars and is ready to claim her under the new law—with the help of his
four brothers—she steals their boat and escapes to the high seas.
Unfortunately, her runaway bid for freedom doesn't last long.

3. https://janspringerauthor.files.wordpress.com/2010/07/alphaoutlaws_js_box_final.jpg

Quickly capturing his lover, Jude rekindles the flames and seduces Cate back into his bed.

But Jude holds a secret that could make him lose Cate forever...

PLUS

The Claiming

Seeking refuge from the Claiming Law, Callie Callahan hides in a deserted cabin in the Maine woods and is shocked when her ex-flame finds her. She's always craved being in Luke Outlaw's arms. Tasting him. Touching him. Taking him deeply within her. So, what's a girl to do but to delve into the sinful delights he offers.

Luke has finally reunited with the love of his life. He knows there is only one way to keep Callie safe and with him forever. He'll do it with the help of his three brothers and an assortment of naughty toys.

Rekindling the flames between them, he unleashes Callie's sensual side, taking her in ways she never dreamed possible, all with the ultimate goal of introducing her to the Outlaw Lovers and The Claiming.

Alpha Outlaws Boxed Set Con't

Colter's Revenge

Revenge belongs to Dr. Colter Outlaw when he unexpectedly reunites with the beautiful woman who broke his heart during the Terrorist Wars. Capturing her, collaring her and holding her against her will, he seduces her, fills her with wicked desires and naughty cravings for a delicious ménage. Fully intent on breaking her heart and walking away, Colter's plans unravel when he submits to the carnal pleasures Ashley gives him so freely.

Colter had told her he loved her. He'd whispered promises of rescue from her life as a slave, but when he'd suddenly disappeared, she'd been devastated. Infected with a version of the X-virus that leaves Ashley Blakely sexually excited on a daily basis, she has come to Pleasure Palace to bid on a cure for her illness. She never expected her Outlaw Lover to be there and screw her plans. Nor did she expect to give him her heart and body so easily...

Tyler's Woman
For years Tyler Outlaw and his best friend, Hunter Brown, endured brutal torture and worse in an overseas terrorist prison. Finally, free of their hell, they return home intent on seducing Laurie into their erotic filled fantasies.
Laurie Callahan has always experienced red-hot pleasure and passionate love in Tyler Outlaw's arms. But when he's pronounced MIA, presumed dead in the Terrorist Wars, Laurie's world is shattered, and her heart is broken.
Shocked to discover Tyler is alive and he's taken a male lover, Laurie is thrust into a sensual world of sizzling seductions, scorching ménages and the carnal desires that both scarred men crave. But she fears Tyler won't want her when he discovers she's not the same woman he left behind...
****READER CAUTION IS ADVISED (m/m forced scenes) ****

Resistance
In the near future, a virus has been unleashed, killing a majority of the world's female population, forcing the introduction of the Claiming Law. A law that states men have all the rights and women are sexual property claimable by groups of men.
Fugitive female...

Renegade Resistance leader Reena "Red" Wilde is in for the fight of her life when she experiences an erotic attraction to the two most dangerous men she's ever met.

Black ops assassin...

Months ago, Will "Blade" Smith spent one sizzling evening in the arms of a red-haired seductress. Now she's his next assignment. One look into her gorgeous eyes and he's wrestling his heated cravings for her all over again.

Bounty Hunter...

When Cade Outlaw nabs his bounty, sexy-as-sin Reena Wilde, his profession dictates she's hands-off. But he can't ignore the magnetic sparks between them...or that she is the biggest temptation of his life.

Resistance is futile...

After Reena escapes Cade and Will and falls prey to a band of evil hunters, she's grateful her sexy hunks come to her rescue...and in return, saves their lives. Trapped in a solitary cabin during a wicked snowstorm, she can't resist her two, well-hung studs, nor can she deny they've claimed her heart.

Many more Jasmine Black and Jan Springer eBooks, print books, audiobooks plus translated eBooks and print books can be found at http://www.janspringer.com and http://www.jasmine-black.com

Here are ways we can connect:

Jasmine Black Website at http://janspringerauthor.wordpress.com/
jasmine-black/
Jan Springer Website at http://www.janspringer.com[1]
Instagram – http://www.instagram.com/janspringerauthor
Facebook - https://www.facebook.com/janspringereroticromance
Twitter Jan Springer- https://twitter.com/janspringer @janspringer
Twitter Jasmine Black - https://twitter.com/blackerotica1
@blackerotica1
Pinterest - http://www.pinterest.com/janspringer1/
Jan's Blog - http://janspringerauthor.wordpress.com/blog-2/
Happy Reading,
Jasmine Black / Jan Springer

---

1. http://www.janspringer.com/

Don't miss out!

Visit the website below and you can sign up to receive emails whenever Jasmine Black publishes a new book. There's no charge and no obligation.

https://books2read.com/r/B-A-GIJD-MURDC

BOOKS 2 READ

Connecting independent readers to independent writers.